ADIRONDACK FAIRY TALES

Lettie A. Petrie

D1089535

North Country Books
Utica, New York

ADIRONDACK FAIRY TALES

Copyright © 1996
by
Lettie A. Petrie

SECOND PRINTING 2001

Characterization by
Lettie A. Petrie
with
Kathryn Mowry and John Mahaffy

ISBN 0-925168-53-X

Library of Congress Cataloging-in-Publication Data

Petrie, Lettie A., 1924 -
   Read-aloud Adirondack fairy tales / Lettie A. Petrie
    p. cm.
   Contents: Bob—Marshmallow—Buffy—Buffy's
adventure—Dudley—Oscar's pie—The year of the bear.
   ISBN 0-925168-53-X
   1. Children's stories, American. [1. Short stories. 2.
Animals-Fiction.] I. Title.
PZ7.P44678Re   1996
[Fic]—dc20   96-8038
                                 CIP
                                 AC

North Country Books, Inc.
311 Turner Street
Utica, New York 13501

Dedication

*This book is for my children, my grandchildren,
my family, and my friends who have all shared
the wonders of the Adirondacks with me.
It is also in loving memory of my husband,
who first took us there, and for my daughter,
Susey, who loved the mountains and
every animal who lived there all of her life.*

Bob

For many years a small, brown-striped chipmunk has lived in his hole under a big tree at a campground in the Adirondack Mountains.

He is an adventurous little chipmunk who likes to squirm into garbage cans looking for nuts.

One day the lid of a can came down with a crash, taking off the tip of his bushy tail. After that campers called him "Bob" because of his bobbed, stubby tail.

Bob's campground is at the edge of a deep woods, on the shore of a small lake. Families come from miles around to spend their vacations, and they look for Bob when they come.

He scampers around eagerly taking the nuts they offer. He likes these humans who hold scraps of food for him to take. He stuffs peanuts into his cheeks before running back to store them in his hole.

Marshmallow

There are rabbits, squirrels, raccoons and lots of other small animals at this lake, as well as a few BIG black bears! One extra-large bear seems to like campers just as much as Bob does.

He comes out of the woods as darkness creeps in. He stands up on his hind legs, begging for marshmallows being roasted over the campfires. Sometimes the marshmallows stick to his fur as he puts his front paws up to pop them into his mouth.

Bob calls him "Marshmallow." He likes him.

Marshmallow is always careful not to step on Bob as he scampers along beside him.

One day Marshmallow was lured into a big round drum with smelly food inside—a bear trap! The door came crashing down, trapping him. Bob snuck in to be with his friend. He was afraid but he stayed, hidden in the straw. He wanted to know where Marshmallow was going.

Forest Rangers hauled him to the big dump on the edge of town. They took the big bears away because some of the campers were afraid of them. The dump bears live in the forest, coming out at night to feed in the big pit where garbage is dumped every day.

Bob sadly said good-bye to his friend.

Buffy

There is a magical place in the Adirondack Mountains called Buttermilk Falls. It is just a few miles outside the village of Long Lake. High waterfalls cascade over big flat rocks, slowing as they reach a gentle slope, and ending in a small, still pool. In the deep woods around the falls there is a quiet glen where tender green grass grows and the air is filled with the fragrance of pine trees. Only a small dirt road leads into this place that time forgot.

Buffy is a Snowshoe rabbit who was born there in the glen in early Spring. Even before she could open her round, black eyes she could smell the sweet grass and the wildflowers that were pushing their way into the world. She is light brown, with white feet and a tiny powder-puff tail, like her brother, Benji, and her sister, Maisie. Her mother, Abigail, will turn the same shade of light brown as the weather warms and the brown earth loses its winter coat of snow.

Next winter Buffy and her family will again be white so they can hide in the snow from their enemies, just as they blend with the earth during the summer months.

A few days after she was born, Buffy's eyes
opened to her new world, and she wiggled her nose
happily, hopping out of her cozy burrow. Already, her
hind feet were much longer than her front. She was
able to take big jumps when she wanted to hurry.
Buffy had one ear that flopped instead of standing
straight. Benji, teased her about it, calling her "Buffy
Flopear." He teased her so much that other rabbits
called her that too, but Buffy didn't really mind.

Hidden in the grass that grew higher and thicker as the weather grew warmer, she often watched a mother deer bring her little spotted fawn to the water to drink every morning just after dawn. Buffy loved to sit quietly while raccoons came to the lake to wash their food holding it in their black paws before eating the tender green shoots. Her mother said they did that to clean their food.

When Buffy dragged a long leaf to the edge of the lake, thinking she would wash it, she almost tumbled into the water. She didn't have long finger-like raccoon claws. She tried everything she saw other animals do. The world was so exciting! Each night, snuggled close to her mother, she was lulled to sleep by the soft murmur of the falls.

Buffy's Adventure

One warm, sunny day Buffy hopped out of her burrow and her heart jumped! There was a huge creature standing near the edge of the water. This giant was covered with long, dark red hair. Looking up in wonder, Buffy saw big brown eyes and a huge mouth. WHAT WAS IT? She wanted to hide, but she was too late. He saw her! He moved slowly towards her. She gasped.

He was almost as tall as the fawn she watched every day! His fur was dark red, and he had a long, shaggy tail, that wagged back and forth as his brown eyes looked at her. Buffy sat there on her hind legs, afraid to move.

"You are scaring her, Morgan. Sit!" Another tall creature! This one Buffy recognized as a human.

Buffy wished her mother and her brother and sister were here! She didn't know what to do! SHOULD SHE TRY TO HOP AWAY? No, they would catch her if she did. They were too close.

"This is my dog, and I'm Susey We won't hurt
you."

Her dog? What is a dog? Buffy's curiosity got the
best of her and she hopped a little closer.

"We came to have a picnic. Would you like to
share it with us?"

Buffy didn't know what to do. She sat still as the human reached into her bag and brought out a package. It smelled good! Susey held something white, with green leaves poking out the side. Breaking off a piece, she laid it on the ground between them, and held out another piece to the red dog. He quickly ate it, wagging his tail.

Buffy cautiously started to nibble on the green leaf. IT WAS CRISP AND DELICIOUS! She forgot to be afraid and chewed happily, moving closer. Susey sat with her legs stretched out, watching Buffy eat. The dog moved closer to Buffy and his big tail wagged so hard it knocked her right into the water!

HELP! She could feel the cold water all around her.

Just as she began to sink below the wet, dark surface, she felt something grasp the loose skin behind her small head. The dog had her in his mouth! HE'S GOING TO EAT ME! MAMA! Sure she was going to die, she closed her eyes, but some warm hands took her from Morgan's mouth.

Susey wiped Buffy with a soft white cloth. "There. Don't be scared. He wouldn't hurt you."

The dog lapped her, right across her floppy ear. HE REALLY WAS NOT TRYING TO EAT HER! Buffy lay quietly in Susey's lap as she rubbed her fur dry. It felt wonderful! Before long, she put Buffy back on the grass and gave her another leaf.

That summer, as Buffy grew bigger, Susey and Morgan came back often, bringing Buffy lettuce and carrots. She was always glad to see them, but she was careful to stay away from that cold water, and from the red dog's swishing tail!

Dudley

Once upon a time a little Mallard Duck named Dudley was born in the Adirondack Mountains, at Fourth Lake.

He lives with his two brothers, three sisters, his mother and his father near the village of Old Forge. It is a beautiful place, near many lakes and rivers.

Dudley thinks his father is handsome. He has a dark green head and a white collar around his neck. His bill is deep yellow, and he has sharp black eyes. His feathers are brown and gray, and the edge of each big wing has bright blue feathers, with black and white bands. His tail feathers have white tips, and his webbed feet are orange. He swims alone most of the time, but he visits with his family every day. Dudley is glad he and his two brothers will look like their father someday.

Every day Dudley swims behind his mother with his brothers and sisters. He likes to go fast, and he often gets ahead of her, swimming away by himself to explore the big lake. When he does that, his mother scolds him. "Dudley, there are big fish in this lake who eat little ducks when they are alone. You stay right behind me!"

He often forgets his mother's warning. Dudley loves to swim close to the shore where he can see people sitting on the sandy beach. He likes to sun himself on the warm stones near the water's edge.

People throw him bread crusts. He gobbles them up as fast as he can before some other duck gets them. His mother quacks loudly, scolding him when she catches him near the shore. "Someday you will be sorry you are so naughty."

One beautiful summer afternoon, when the sun shone warmly on the sparkling blue water, Dudley just had to explore. He was having a fine old time, forgetting all about his mother as he looked at the glittering white sand. It twinkled like thousands of little diamonds. The green shade trees called to him and he drifted even closer to the shore.

Suddenly, he felt something pulling on his foot! It was a FISH! Dudley was scared! He pulled, and pulled, but the fish had Dudley's foot in its mouth and he could feel himself being pulled under the water!

"Mama! Help me!" He quacked and quacked, struggling mightily, but she was too far away to hear him. Dudley tried to stay on top of the water. "Help! Help!" he quacked.

"I'm coming! Hold on!" It was his father—just in time! He dove under the water and chased the hungry fish away. Dudley swam close to his father, trembling with fear. He was glad to see him!

"Why are you by yourself?" his father quacked sternly. "Why aren't you with your mother?"

His mother, hearing the commotion, swam as fast as she could to reach her son. "Dudley! Dudley, how many times must I tell you not to leave me?"

"I'll never leave you again, Mama," he promised. "That fish almost got me!"

By the time they are ready to fly to other feeding grounds, Dudley will be big enough to take care of himself, but until then, he won't leave his mother's side again.

He learned a lesson he will never forget!

Oscar's Pie

Oscar Longears wiggled his brown nose. His big black eyes looked up into the branches of the maple tree shading his home.

Fall had come early to the Adirondack Mountains. The crisp, cold air near the village of Speculator was filled with the scent of freshly cut hay. Leaves were steadily falling, covering the ground around him in a red and gold carpet.

On one of the lowest branches of a maple tree he could see Mrs. Wren, busily giving her nest a last cleaning before going south for the winter.

Suddenly Oscar's nose twitched. WHAT WAS THAT WONDERFUL SMELL? He turned and looked. His mother, Matilda Longears, had just placed three luscious squash pies on the windowsill! That was what he smelled!

His family had worked all through the long, hot summer to store carrots, parsnips and acorn squash to feed them during the winter. Papa Benjamin Longears insisted they all help with the work before they played.

Sometimes Oscar and his brother, Jerry, resented that, but now, looking at their full pantry, he was happy. Except that he had not had a squash pie all summer . . .

Noticing his father and brother whispering near the door to their burrow, Oscar cautiously sneaked behind them and took the nearest pie! Holding it carefully, he quietly crept away.

He hopped down the gravel path to the edge of the freshly mown meadow, and set his precious burden on a big flat rock. He could hardly wait to taste that pie! I DESERVE THIS TREAT. I'VE WORKED ALL SUMMER, he thought, and tried not to feel guilty. It was a beautiful pie, all golden brown and juicy with squash. His mouth watered.

Oscar was so busy thinking about how good his first bite would taste that he didn't hear his father and brother. His heart jumped as he discovered them just behind him— and to his surprise, he saw each of them carried a pie!

"They smell wonderful, don't they!" Benjamin Longears smiled. "I'm sure your mother would want Jerry and I to have these two pies as long as you took one for yourself." He set his pie carefully beside Oscar's, and Jerry put his down next to them.

"What about Mama? Shouldn't we save some for her?" Oscar was suddenly full of doubt. It was one thing to take ONE pie, but not to leave some for Mama seemed kind of mean.

"Do you think we should? You must have thought it was all right when you took your pie. What's the difference—one pie or three?" Papa Longears looked at him thoughtfully.

"How did you know I took it? I was really quiet."

Oscar pretended he didn't hear his father's question.

"Freddie Fieldmouse saw you, and he told Mama," Jerry answered, grinning.

"You mean Mama knows I took the pie?"

Now Oscar really felt terrible. His mother never took anything without permission. She even asked Farmer Peters for the old, left-over vegetables he threw out of his garden.

"Your mother knows," his father said quietly. "What do you think we should do?"

Oscar thought hard. "I think we should take all the pies back and share them with Mama. She worked all summer, and she made the pies."

"Are you sure you want to do that? You don't want a whole pie for yourself?" Papa Longears' eyes twinkled.

"I'm sure!"

Oscar picked up his pie and his father and brother
followed him back to their burrow. In their cozy
kitchen, his mother had the table set for four.

"Back from your walk with the pies? Are they cool
enough to eat now?" She smiled. She was not really
surprised Oscar had decided to share his pie.

Because she didn't approve of mice on her table, Matilda put Freddie Fieldmouse's pie atop a leaf on the floor.

She called to Dottie Wren to be sure and pick up the crumbs on the sill before she left on her trip south That night they all slept soundly, their stomachs full of squash pie, and Oscar dreamed of all the pies they would share that winter.

The Year of the Bear

Not so long ago there came a time that campers remember as "THE YEAR OF THE BEAR!" People who lived in town near the campground decided to cover the dump and make it a landfill—a place to store waste safely. Soon, the bears could not find enough food.

They started to wander, and many of them found
their way back to the campground where they knew
those garbage cans could still be found!

Suddenly, there were a LOT of bears near Bob's clearing! He was happy to see Marshmallow again, but as those other big bears grew bolder, he stayed away from them.

Bears are always hungry, and while they usually sleep all day, being "nocturnal" or "night" creatures by instinct, now they began to roam in the daytime. It became a common sight to see a bear in the middle of the afternoon, lumbering down the road near the campground, looking for food. Their empty stomachs growling. "Gr-rr!"

Some bears, smelling food inside campers' tents and screened-rooms, tore their way in and ripped open food lockers and coolers. Park Rangers tried to warn the humans to keep their food in safe places, but many of them didn't. Bob didn't get many nuts that year. Campers, afraid of the bears, packed up and went home.

That winter the animals were so hungry they didn't sleep very well. When Spring came, the garbage cans were gone! Big drums looking like bear-traps were all around the park. Hungry bears couldn't rip them open when they smelled food inside. DUMPSTERS has replaced the cans they loved! Most of the bears were tricked into bear-traps again, and Rangers hauled them away to woods far from the lake. But not Marshmallow. He found food and stayed with Bob at the campground.

Bob still sits with children while his picture is taken. He brings treats to his friend, Marshmallow, who is a smarter bear now. He leaves those traps alone and looks for food in the woods, only taking marshmallows when offered.

If you were to visit the campground you might see Bob, and he would tell you, if he could, "The Year of the Bear" was something to tell your grandchildren about!

Elroy, the Adirondack Moose

Elroy wandered down a shady road circling the Lake Eaton campgrounds. He was tired! He was hungry! He was discouraged!

When he was born, high in these mountains, in a place called Lake Placid, he and his mother were the only moose around. His mother explained that moose mostly live in a place called Canada, even farther north than Lake Placid. His father left them to go back to Canada where the weather suited him better. Now his mother said it was time for Elroy to be on his own.

He walked, sniffing the fresh mountain air, looking at the sparkling blue waters of the lake, surrounded by lofty pine trees. Suddenly, Elroy heard a "squeak!" He looked down and, to his surprise, saw a small, brown-striped chipmunk, with a short bobbed tail. He was sitting on his hind legs, looking at him with wide, round, black eyes. "Wow! What kind of animal are you?"

"I'm a moose," Elroy answered.

"A moose? What are you doing here?"

"I'm looking for a friend." He looked hopeful. "Do you have other moose here?"

"Gosh, I really don't know! But wait! We could ask Marshmallow. He's a bear who lives here. He might have seen a moose before." The little chipmunk ran ahead. "Come on. I'll take you to him."

"Mama says bears are my enemy," Elroy objected.

"Not Marshmallow," the chipmunk assured him. "He only eats berries and marshmallows and things like that."

Marshmallow was sleeping under a big pine tree deep in the woods behind Lake Eaton. It was a warm, sunny day, and he liked to sleep until the sun went down and the stars came out. That was the time campers sat around their fires and fed him marshmallows when he begged for them.

He opened one sleepy eye when Bob ran up and tugged on his ear. When he saw Elroy looking down at him, he was suddenly wide awake!

"Bob! Why have you brought a moose to my den?"
He was indignant.

"This is Elroy. He's my friend," Bob explained.
"He's looking for a girl moose to be his mate. Have
you seen any moose near here?"

Marshmallow thought for a minute. "No, I've never seen anything like him around here. I did see a deer when I came through Saranac Lake. I guess you'll have to go down the mountain. You might find a girl moose lower in the hills."

Reluctantly Elroy agreed. He wandered through the woods until, late that night, he reached a beautiful little glen by a high waterfall, and wearily he fell asleep.

When he woke, the next thing he saw was a little rabbit.

"What kind of animal are you?" the rabbit asked cautiously.

"I'm a moose." Elroy was getting tired of explaining. Didn't anyone know what a moose was? "I'm looking for a girl moose. Have you seen one?"

"You are at Buttermilk Falls, and I don't think we have moose here. I'm Buffy. We have some pretty deer. Would that help?"

He shook his big head. "No. Deer are not the same as me. I have to find another moose." He was embarrassed.

"Well, you're not going to find one here," Buffy said. "I guess you'll have to go down the mountain."

All day Elroy wandered. Sometimes he got quite close to a winding road with cars whizzing along at a terrific speed. They scared him! Whenever he saw one, he ran back into the woods. As it started to get dark, he came to a place where he could see a big lake, but there were streets everywhere—and those strange, two-legged creatures his Mama called humans!

He created quite a stir as he walked down the street, looking at the shiny glass windows! Everyone shouted. "Look! A moose! A moose right here in Old Forge!" Elroy ran as fast as he could! They scared him!

He saw a patch of woods near the lake, and he ran
into them and went carefully down a path leading to
the water. There, on the rocky shore, was a family of
Mallard ducks. One of them came boldly near him.
"Hi!" the little duck quacked. "Are you a deer?"

"No," Elroy said, in a resigned voice. "I'm a moose. I don't suppose you've seen one before, have you?"

"No! My name is Dudley. I'm a Mallard duck, and I've never seen anyone like you. Let me ask my mother. She's seen just about everything here at Fourth Lake."

Elroy waited anxiously. Dudley waddled back. "Mama says there are no moose here. She says you should live in a place called Canada." Dudley cocked his head. "Why are you here?"

"I'm looking for a girl moose." Elroy was getting tired of explaining. "I guess I'll have to go farther down the mountain."

The nights were getting colder, and the leaves on the big trees were starting to turn shades of orange, scarlet and yellow, dropping to make a carpet of bright colors. Elroy's instincts told him he had to hurry.

He reached the Erie Canal and a place called Rome late in the afternoon. He wandered out of the woods into a meadow where he could eat from the green berry bushes along its edges, and down the towpath next to the canal. He could smell other animals in the air around the canal. There were big barges floating along the dark water, pulled by teams of big animals that made his heart pound excitedly. Humans on the boats shouted when they saw Elroy, but he paid no attention. He moved closer. They were not like him either. Where, oh where, was there another moose?

The next day, as he ambled along, he could see a huge city in the distance, and cars whizzed along the highway at a dizzying speed! He had trouble finding woods where he could hide. Humans sighted him from their cars. "A moose in Syracuse! I can't believe it!" A white-haired woman rolled down her window as she and her husband stopped their car to stare when Elroy walked shyly out of the woods.

I've got to change my direction, Elroy decided, sniffing the breeze. He turned and headed north, away from the big city. That night he found a pasture with

some black and white cows in it. He liked them. But they didn't seem to like him! They all bunched up together when he approached and wouldn't let him near them. "I'm looking for another moose—a cow moose," he explained.

"I'm not a moose. And these other girls are not moose either," the closest one mooed. Feeling hopeless, he turned away and slept under a big old maple tree.

The next morning he plodded along, passing a city called Watertown. He knew he was getting closer to home. There was something about the air! Along wooded paths everything looked familiar. Suddenly, he knew where he was! He was back in Lake Placid! Eagerly, he looked for his mother. She was not there, but. . . . he walked, as quietly as a big moose can, and there—just ahead was a beautiful, young moose! Shyly, she lowered her lashes over her big eyes.

"My name is Belle. I'm so glad to see you. I've been so lonesome."

He touched her with his muzzle. "I'm Elroy. I'm lonely too." Together they walked into the sunset. Home at last!